A Note to Parents and Caregivers:

Read-it! Readers are for children who are just starting on the amazing road to reading. These beautiful books support both the acquisition of reading skills and the love of books.

 The PURPLE LEVEL presents basic topics and objects using high frequency words and simple language patterns.

 The RED LEVEL presents familiar topics using common words and repeating sentence patterns.

 The BLUE LEVEL presents new ideas using a larger vocabulary and varied sentence structure.

 The YELLOW LEVEL presents more challenging ideas, a broad vocabulary, and wide variety in sentence structure.

 The GREEN LEVEL presents more complex ideas, an extended vocabulary range, and expanded language structures.

 The ORANGE LEVEL presents a wide range of ideas and concepts using challenging vocabulary and complex language structures.

When sharing a book with your child, read in short stretches, pausing often to talk about the pictures. Have your child turn the pages and point to the pictures and familiar words. And be sure to reread favorite stories or parts of stories.

There is no right or wrong way to share books with children. Find time to read with your child, and pass on the legacy of literacy.

Adria F. Klein, Ph.D.
Professor Emeritus
California State University
San Bernardino, California

Editor: Christianne Jones
Designer: Hilary Wacholtz
Art Director: Nathan Gassman
The illustrations in this book were created with watercolor and pencil.

Picture Window Books
1710 Roe Crest Drive
P.O. Box 669
North Mankato, MN 56003-0669
877-845-8392
www.picturewindowbooks.com

Printed in the United States of America in North Mankato, Minnesota.
052012
006702R

Library of Congress Cataloging-in-Publication Data
Klein, Adria F. (Adria Fay), 1947-
Max goes to the fire station / by Adria F. Klein ; illustrated by
Mernie Gallagher-Cole.
p. cm. — (Read-it! readers. The life of Max)
ISBN 978-1-4048-5266-2 (hardcover)
[1. Fire departments—Fiction. 2. Hispanic Americans—Fiction.] I. Gallagher-Cole,
Mernie, ill. II. Title.
PZ7.K678324Mas 2009
[E]—dc22
                                    2008030890

Max
Goes to the
Fire Station

by Adria F. Klein
illustrated by Mernie Gallagher-Cole

Special thanks to our reading adviser:

Susan Kesselring, M.A., Literacy Educator
Rosemount–Apple Valley–Eagan (Minnesota) School District

PICTURE WINDOW BOOKS
Minneapolis, Minnesota

Max and his class are at the
fire station.

Firefighters help people. They try to keep everyone safe.

Many firefighters live at the fire station while they work. They eat and sleep there.

The fire chief talks about fire safety.

Never leave candles burning. And
never play with matches.

Then he talks about campfire
safety. Always make sure the
campfire is out.

First pour water on it. Then shovel
dirt on it.

Max and his class see two big fire engines.

They also see one small fire truck.

The firefighters show the class how to hold the big fire hose.

The firefighters put the hose on one of the big fire trucks.

The fire chief shows the class what the firefighters wear.

They see the fire hat, fire gloves, fire boots, and a special coat.

The fire chief sounds the fire alarm.
It is very loud!

A firefighter slide down a big pole.

Max tells Don he wants to be
a firefighter.

Don says he wants to be a firefighter, too.

After the field trip, Max draws a picture of a firefighter.

He had lots of fun at the fire station.